The Little Fisherman's Catch

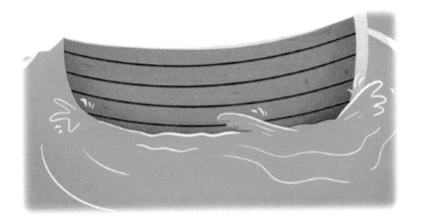

This book belongs to:

_____

WRITTEN BY JUSTINE. J. AUGUST

Dedicated to my three beautiful children,
Savannah, Saharah and Andrew.

"I Can Do All Things Through Christ Who Strengthens Me". Philippians 14:3 KJV

In a small village called Maskall lived a family of three; a father and his two children. His oldest was a son called Troy and his daughter was called Lela.

The father was a very poor fisherman who used the little money he made from selling his fishes to send his two children to school.

Troy didn't like school as much as Lela and did very poorly in school. He wanted to be a fisherman like his father. Lela was very smart and did extremely well in school.

The father would often reward Lela with little tokens to show her how proud he was of her.

Troy was so sure he wanted to be a fisherman that he stopped going to school and offered to go with his father to help him.

Even though his father didn't want him to come out of school, he still agreed to take Troy along with him to fish.

Troy was very happy because his dream of becoming a fisherman was finally coming true.

The father was very sad because he didn't want his son to become a poor fisherman like him and have to struggle.

So, the father quickly thought of a plan to discourage Troy from becoming a fisherman and going back to school.

Troy was very excited for his first day of fishing. Determined to discourage his son, the father took him to a part of the river where he knew there weren't many fishes.

After they got settled both Troy and his father casted their fishing rods into the river.

Troy held his fishing rod firmly waiting patiently to catch his first fish. They stayed there all day and caught no fishes. Troy said, "Father, why is it taking so long for us to catch a fish?"

His father replied, "That's how it is son, some days are good and some days you go home empty, but we will try again tomorrow."

The next day Troy and his father went out again and after a long day they only caught two fishes that were very small.

Troy and his father did this for a week with very little catch.

The father was very happy because he thought his plan was working to discourage Troy from becoming a fisherman and he would eventually go back to school.

However, Troy was still not discouraged. One morning Troy got up very early, packed up his fishing gears and set off on his own in his father's canoe.

On his way he saw some other fisherman and greeted them. One of the fishermen asked, "Where are you going boy?"

He pointed to the direction where his father usually took him and replied, " Over there sir, that's where my father and I go to fish."

The fishermen all laughed at him and said "You won't catch a thing there boy, even your father knows that!" Troy was confused because his father took him there for a week.

Troy was sad that his father had been taking him to a fishing area where he knew there weren't any fishes.

He soon realized that his father was just trying to discourage him. "Go home boy, before you catch a cold!" one of the other fishermen shouted as he laughed and paddled away.

Determined to prove to his father and the other fishermen wrong, Troy continued on his way.

He quietly followed the other fishermen from a distance to a different fishing area. The fishermen went left and Troy paddled to the far right where he saw a small little mangrove island in the river.

He was all alone except for the birds that would occasionally fly down to fish.

At first Troy was very doubtful about fishing by the little island because he was all alone, and no one seemed to go there.

He thought to himself that perhaps none of the fishermen went there because it wasn't a good fishing spot like the one his father took him. But Troy was determined so he placed a worm on the hook and cast his rod into the river just as his father taught him.

First, he felt a small tug on his fishing rod. Then, he felt a much stronger pull. Troy had a big fish on his line. Troy pulled and he pulled, but the fish kept jumping and splashing. But Troy kept on going until he finally got it inside his little canoe.

He caught his first big fish. He was so happy and excited. So, again Troy cast his line and again he caught another big fish. It started to rain and Troy had forgotten to pack his raincoat.

"I'm going to catch a cold for sure" Troy exclaimed. But Troy continued fishing until his little canoe was filled with fishes.

He grew very cold and started coughing, his clothes were soaking wet.

His hands also became very sore and tired, pulling in all the fishes. By accident, Troy had discovered the best fishing spot in the entire river. The fishes there were far bigger than fishes anywhere else in the river. Troy decided that he had caught enough fish for one day, and he was very cold and tired.

He needed to save the rest of his energy to paddle back inland. And so, Troy began his journey home, paddling very slowly.

On his way down the river, he ran into the same fishermen that laughed at him earlier.

They were completely unaware that little Troy had found the best fishing spot and had so many fishes. One of the fishermen chuckled and yelled, "Looked like he caught something after all." Another yelled, "probably a cold from being out here in the rain!" They all laughed at him and went on their way. But Troy was too exhausted to respond. The fishermen all took their catch to the market to sell.

There was a huge crowd around a stall but none of the other fishermen knew who it was attracting such a large crowd. In all the years they have never seen such a huge crowd in front of one stall.

Very curious, one fisherman went to find out what was going on. As he got closer, he saw people walking away with large fishes. He hurried back to the other fishermen and yelled "Come! Come and see the size of these fishes this fisherman is selling!"

Maskall village was so small that it was long before Troy's father heard about the fisherman who was selling big fishes at the market. All the other fishermen hurried to see which fisherman it was, but it was too crowded to see.

When most of the fish were sold and the crowd got smaller, one fisherman was able to see who it was selling the big fish. "It's the boy, it's the boy!" he yelled shockingly. The other fishermen felt so ashamed and didn't say a word to Troy. They all just looked at him in disbelief. That day none of the other fishermen sold all their fishes because their fishes were much smaller than Troy's. Troy went home with a large sum of money he had made from selling the fishes.

He had sold all the fishes except for one that he saved to take home for his father. "Here father, I saved a fish for you from my catch today." His father was surprised at the large size of the fish.

"It was you everyone was talking about with all the big fishes. It was my son!" Troy sobbed and replied "Yes father it was me. I found a new fishing spot with lots of big fishes." His father felt so ashamed and told him what he had done to discourage him from being a fisherman.

"I'm so sorry son!" His father exclaimed, "I just want you to stay in school, but you are a better fisherman than me."

Tory was very sick because of the cold he had caught while he was out fishing in the rain. Coughing and sneezing, Troy said, "It's ok father, I really don't want to be a fisherman anymore."

His father was surprised. "But you are already a fisherman's son, look at how much money you made today!" Troy had more money that his father made in a month of selling his fishes.

"I will go back to school father. I want to become a doctor so I can find a cure for the cold." His father laughed with joy. Troy kept coughing and sneezing so his father prepared him some hot tea and soup.

Later his father tucked him in bed and told him how proud he was of him.

THE END……..

"Have I not commanded you? Be strong and courageous. Do not be afraid; do not be discouraged, for the LORD your God will be with you wherever you go." Joshua 1:9 NIV

NOTE TO FAMILIES

I have grown up listening and reading a lot of children stories with great morals. I think these stories are still very important to kids today. Especially now, more than ever, where social media has a great impact on how our kids view themselves. Its imminent that we get our kids reading again, discovering new ways to build their confidence instead of depending on likes on social media. Together we can make a difference and raise happy and confident children.

15285569R00035